PRAISE F̶ ̶ ̶ ̶ ̶ ̶ ̶ ̶ ̶ ̶ ̶ ̶ ̶ ̶

Delicious, heady, transporting…

— M.P.

This book made me gasp and laugh, too. Lovely's voice is fresh, intoxicatingly creative and the start of what should be an unforgettable new series…

— LINDSAY EMORY, BOOKS TO READ NOW

If your fancy gets tickled by Leda romping with Zeus-as-swan; if you always secretly thought King Triton was hotter than Prince Eric; if you ever wondered how mer-people have sex; if you like your romance novels with a hearty serving of heroine who is both strong and vulnerable, sexy and intelligent, and who takes her pleasure rather than waiting for it to be served (at which point it's often tepid and spiceless), THIS IS THE BOOK FOR YOU.

— AMAZON 5-STAR REVIEW

This book got me pregnant.

— ANONYMOUS

KING OF THE SEA

A PARANORMAL MERMAN ROMANCE

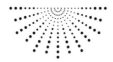

LAURA LOVELY

Editor: Mayumi Shimose Poe

Cover: Romanced by the Cover

❀ Created with Vellum

A GIFT FOR CLEVER BEAUTIES

Hello, you gorgeous creature!

Congratulations on making the excellent decision to pick up this book! Want something special, just for you?

I give exclusive excerpts of new stories and special bonus scenes, only to my newsletter subscribers. Join my email list and I'll send you a special collection!

Here's the link: http://bit.ly/lovelyreaderbonus

You're worth it! xoxo

P.S. I promise you won't get too many emails - I'm too busy having fun to be a bother.

For Alexandra, who requested this story, and for Julia, who held my hand the whole time.

PROLOGUE

A TALE OF TRUE LOVE, ORIGINALLY TOLD IN THE SALON OF MADAME DE BOUDOIR, SIREN AND STORYTELLER.

*B*on soir, bienvenue, *welcome and hello.*

For those of you who don't know, or have had too much champagne to recall, I am Madame de Boudoir, daughter of Aphrodite, chanteuse of the high seas, your hostess for the evening and teller of the fairytales your mother would blush to speak aloud.

They are all true, by the way. My stories. As true as you could want them to be. As true as anything the night can tell. The night can tell a lot of truths, n'est-ce pas? *That is why you will find only candlelight in my salon. It illuminates just the parts you long to see.*

Where are you tonight? If you took the red door, you arrived at the Moulin Rouge. If you took the invisible door, it brought you to me. And here you are.

Aren't we, Raoul? Here. Keep playing. Pianissimo, *Raoul.* Pianissimo.

1

You, handsome, sitting there. Hold my champagne. Kiss my hand, too. C'est bon. *Very good.*

When I was a little girl, I loved to spend my evenings at the seashore and hear the stories my aunts would sing to the moon. They were mermaids, all of them, my aunts. Naturally. My whole family belongs to the sea, and to love. We are the children of the Aphrodite, as I said.

Even the mighty Triton, who lives in a golden palace beneath the waves, is a captive of love. We cannot escape it, although we try. I have escaped enough husbands to know. Isn't that so, handsome? Yes, give me back my glass. Kiss my hand again. Very good. Saluté.

Tonight, as surely as the trail of my gown upon this stage entrances your gaze, my story will entrance your heart.

You may have heard of the showgirl Alexandra La Sirène, the Mermaid of Monte Carlo, the great danseur *of her age. The jewel of Monte Carlo at the dawn of its time.*

What you have not heard is the story of how she gained her skill...and of a love affair that lives outside the bounds of time, of reason, a love that lives both on land and in the sea. A love that could draw even Triton from his lair.

You, ma cher, *look as if you don't believe. But those of us who have seen the sea, we know. When we ponder what mysteries lie in the deep, do we not also look for what mysteries might wash ashore?*

I will speak of love tonight, in great detail. If you ever feel that you cannot look upon the naked face of love, look then upon my gown of gossamer and glass, while I sing you a song, a song of...

THE KING OF THE SEA.

A TREACHEROUS HEART

riton, King of the Sea, surveyed the destruction of his daughter Amarine's secret grotto. Broken teacups, ripped artwork, tangled forks, and smashed figurines lay scattered on the rock floor. All of her treasures, ruined with a single swipe of his explosive trident. Everything she had collected from shipwrecks ever since she was a small fry with a tail that could hardly swish. She had kept these things even though it was forbidden, and he had indulged her. Until she had gone too far. It was one thing to treasure a bit of a broken vase. It was another to have fallen in love with a human.

Amarine's wide eyes glowered at him from behind the stalagmite where she had taken refuge. She swam out to confront him, her green tail twitching with anger. This was not the finest moment of his very long reign as King of the Sea, Defender of the Merfolk, and Guardian of the Golden Palace Beneath the Waves. But how else could he have reacted? He had caught Amarine fresh from not one but two major infractions. First, she had swum to the surface with neither a chaperone nor explicit permission. That alone was

LAURA LOVELY

cause for a severe reprimand. Second, she had returned with neither chagrin nor remorse for causing him a day's worry but, rather, full of...delight. She hadn't noticed the way Triton paced the grotto or the complete relief on his face to see her unharmed. No. She had sauntered right in, as if she'd spent the day collecting seagrass instead of setting off every alarm in the kingdom. And then she had the nerve to ask him for a favor.

Breathless and moon-eyed, she confessed she was in love. With a prince. A *human* prince. Surely, she had pleaded, it would be simple for Triton to override his magical protections and allow her to shift into her land form, even though her eighteenth birthday was two full seasons away. That last part he had barely heard, as his heart lurched so far into his throat he felt strangled. All he could hear was his own fear, thundering through him.

She wanted to leave him.

She loved a human.

A human would hurt her.

She would be lost to him forever.

Humans, Triton knew too well, had boats. And fishing nets. And spears. None of which were as dangerous as the biggest threat of all: a human heart. How in Poseidon's deep blue sea was he supposed to protect his favorite daughter from the treachery of a human heart? A mix of rage and fear had erupted from the tips of his fins, straight out of his trident, which obliterated all of Amarine's treasures with its lighting-like bolts. Everything lay shattered, including his relationship with his daughter.

"How could you?" Amarine's quivering voice darted through the water, piercing Triton's soft, tender papa heart. Amarine was angry and hurt, and it was all his doing.

"It's for your own good," Triton replied. He struggled to inject some gentleness into his steely tone. "I know you can't understand, but I am your father, and your king, and it is my job to protect you."

"*You* understand nothing," Amarine's voice grew louder. "All I want is my own power, which *you* have kept from me."

"You don't understand. It's too dangerous."

"I don't need your protection. I don't need *you*. Get out!" she screamed.

"Amarine—"

"Get out!" Amarine's eyes glowed fire-bright. She reminded him of how her mother had looked when she was angry, as if she could have spit a fireball through water.

Triton turned swiftly, whipping his way through the tunnels of the sea-cave. His fists shook with outrage. His heart thundered in his chest at what she'd driven him to do. He'd hurt the person who meant the most to him, and worst off all, he'd *had* to do it.

Triton launched himself out of the tunnel and into the clearer water above the kelp field that separated this sea-mountain from his palace. Amarine's soft sobs followed him. A school of fish parted, giving him a wide berth as he swam furiously faster. Raising six young mermaids on his own, he thought he had seen everything. He was used to pouting, scheming, tantrums, and all manner of pranks and devilry. Six high-spirited mermaid princesses, each un-mated, would be a challenge for any parent, let alone a king with an underwater kingdom to run. What he wasn't prepared for was his youngest, dearest daughter's flagrant disobedience of his most absolute law. Contact between the human world and the mer-world was forbidden. The punishment was banishment. But the last mermaid Triton would ever want to banish was this daughter.

The horrified look in Amarine's eyes as he had pointed his trident and summoned his power came back to him. Did she think he *wanted* to destroy things she loved? Did she think he *liked* it? Possibly. Young mermaids had a habit of believing the world was stacked against them. He knew, because he lived with six of them. At times, the oppressive weight of a palace full of teenage emotions made him feel like a hermit crab who had picked the wrong shell. He commanded the whole ocean, but only his own daughters could make him feel like entire sea was weighing down on him.

Feelings, he thought. That was the whole problem. Foolish, irresponsible *feelings*. Amarine had said she *loved* a human. Impossible. Triton's stomach flipped at the idea of losing his daughter to a human. It was bad enough to think he might one day lose her to a merman, but a human? He'd sooner leave her in the hands of the Kraken.

Humans were unspeakably cruel. Not to mention stupid and brash. They behaved as if the sea had no rules, as if they could go wherever they pleased, as if they were the ones who ruled the sea. Once, humans had respect for his power, dedicated statues and towns to him and the other elemental deities, repeated stories of how he raised tempests with a flick of his tail. They had lost that respect as they built bigger boats and traveled further. If their eyes landed on a part of the world, they thought they owned it and everything that lived there. If they couldn't kill it, they took it as a pet.

Memory flickered at him. A cascade of long hair, bewitching eyes, a cave guarded by a waterfall, a small inlet that fed into a secret lagoon. Himself as a young merman, enchanted by a long pair of legs that were unfortunately attached to a very human heart. A very cruel human heart, one who took his gifts of precious pearls and adoration and then led her three burly brothers to their secret lagoon, harpoons in hand, ready to make a big catch. It was only his golden trident and the power it could wield that had saved him. He had been younger then, his thick beard and flowing hair had not yet wizened into the silver it was today. It was a lesson he was grateful to learn, that the world above had changed. Humans could no longer be trusted, their awe and respect for the mythical had vanished. Better to retreat to the calmer waters of his kingdom. Better to stick with his own kind. Never again trust a human. Never again love a human. Even if her hair smelled like the wind while she pressed her breasts against him. It was too dangerous.

If loving a human was too hazardous for the King of the Sea, it was beyond perilous for his children. After that near-escape, Triton had set his decree: merfolk were forbidden to interact with humans in any way. When his daughters were born, he bestowed an extra spell upon them. Unlike the rest of his people, his children were unable to shift into their land forms until after their eighteenth birthday. They could swim along the coasts but were prevented from exploring the shores. He had thought that would grant him enough time to teach them about the dangers above the water's surface. He had not banked on having the most willful daughter in all the seven seas.

The two mer-guards positioned at Triton's pearly gates saluted him as he passed, their armor glinting as brightly as the gold turrets looming above them. The merfolk drifting about the courtyard shrunk away, avoiding the wrath bubbling around him. Calder, his eldest son, born of one Triton's youthful dalliances, glowered at him from a corner. No doubt everyone had seen the sparks flying from Amarine's grotto. Triton cringed with embarrassment, but this swiftly turned to anger. What did any of them know about being a king while raising six young mermaids on his own? None of them had a daughter who was in love with a human. Triton glowered at all of them. How dare they have such minuscule problems!

One of his counselors, Maris, a seasoned warrior with a

red-gold tail, was brave enough to approach him. "Your highness, could we move to your private chambers? I have something to discuss with you," she said. On any other day, Triton would have been soothed by Maris's tactful wrangling of his distemper. Usually, he would have set his chin and let Maris follow him to separate wing of the palace, where he could rage in private. That would not work today.

Triton looked around the courtyard at the wide eyes of his subjects, bobbing all around him. He felt every league of the sea that rose above his head. Like an eel trapped inside its hiding hole, he was cornered by his responsibilities. He didn't want to sit on his throne and be watched by big, pleading eyes right now. He didn't want to make fair decisions or listen to the reasoning of his counselors. He wanted action. He wanted to hurt something the way Amarine's disobedience had hurt him.

Triton spun around abruptly, mid-glide. He headed out of the courtyard, pointing his trident so that the gates would slam shut behind him, assuring that no one would follow him. Triton swam quickly through the kelp fields and sea-flower gardens of the palace grounds, away from the shining sea palace that mocked him with its pure, glowing resplendence. It looked like a place where everything was in order, when everything in him was upended.

Triton headed up, up, up, through the murky water, past many a sea creature who knew to clear the way for Triton, King of the Sea. Triton sped faster, and faster, his trident pointed forward, the golden light pulling him to the surface.

He'd find this human with whom Amarine was infatuated. His trident would be like a harpoon, and he'd hurt the man the way Amarine's confession had hurt him. Then nothing in this world, or the one above, could separate him from his daughter. Poseidon help anyone who got in his way.

8

2

A DANGEROUS BEAUTY

"*N*on," said Madame, peering down her long nose at Alexandra's enraged face. "You will not dance tonight."

"I promise, I am ready," protested Alexandra in stilted French, standing up from her dressing room chair. Alexandra took a deep breath, filled with the familiar backstage smells of greasepaint and gaslight. "I know all the choreography. I have rehearsed. I have the costume. You must let me dance." The rest of the dressing room was uncharacteristically silent. None of the other chorus girls wanted to cross Madame, nor did they want to miss a word of this argument.

Madame gave Alexandra a scathing once-over, tapping her finger against the shepherdess hook she had come to retrieve from another dancer. Madame was the costume mistress, den mother, and judicial system all rolled into one. She ruled the dancers and singers of the chorus of the Opéra de Monte Carlo with an iron fist, as if she were Supreme Empress of the backstage. Prince Charles III may be the official champion of the newly built casino and adjoining opera house, but Madame was the one who made it all run. Nothing from the proscenium all the way to the backstage entrance happened without her knowing about it. Every player, from the divas to the sailors moonlighting as scenic riggers, fell in line when she spoke—or else they fell right out of the theater.

Leaning on the doorframe behind Madame's wide skirt, Marie-Louise, the lead chorus girl, chimed in. "She is not trained. She may never be ready." Marie-Louise had been raised in the wings of Paris Opéra Ballet and considered herself the preeminent authority on dance skill. She knew the choreography for every act—and, more valuably, the ins-and-outs of the backstage machinations. *Marie-Louise also knows a few movements they don't teach at the ballet*, thought Alexandra uncharitably. But she couldn't really blame Marie-Louise for entertaining stagedoor suitors. Suitors meant gifts and favors, and that meant survival. Dancing was the first source of income for a showgirl, but it was not the most lucrative.

"It is amazing Monsieur even allowed her in the building, the way she dances." Marie-Louise patted her gleaming blonde hair and smoothed the stiff layers of her white skirt. In Act 1, she played a swan. Alexandra had hoped to make it onstage tonight to at least play a leaf.

"I danced well enough for Monsieur to give me a place in the chorus," said Alexandra. She certainly wasn't going to tell Marie-Louise the truth about her "audition"—that she had talked her way into Monsieur's office and hadn't stopped talking until the manager had agreed to let her join the chorus. On a trial basis, of course. Payment conditional upon her performance, of course. Meaning if Madame wouldn't let her perform, Alexandra wouldn't be paid.

Madame raised an eyebrow high above her painted cheek. "Monsieur is very busy managing the front of house. I run the back of house." Everyone in the opera house knew which dominion was larger, and it wasn't Monsieur's. "But you are new here," continued Madame, "and uneducated in our ways. I am sure in America, you did not have the...benefits of our traditions."

Alexandra wanted to argue that the opera house was less than a year old, that the casino had only just opened to guests, that all of Monte Carlo was still under construction. There were no traditions, which is why she thought she might have a chance here. She hadn't banked on every ambitious performer in Europe lining up first.

"But...I put on a costume," she offered lamely. Nevermind that the costume didn't belong to her. She had plucked it from the racks with the hope that the act of dressing for the part would land her in the part. Or any part.

Subtly, so very subtly, Marie-Louise dragged her hands up her own hips, to rest around her tightly corseted waist. Marie-Louise's waist was the circumference of a pint glass, or so she liked to tell people. Her gesture was a not-so-subtle suggestion that Alexandra's lush frame would never fit in Marie-Louise's swan costume. *No matter,* thought Alexandra, who had no regrets about owning a figure that had more turns than a fouetté series. *The swan's neck does stand out, but it's the rump that makes it glide.*

"Act 1 is set in the spring," said Madame. "The leaves have not yet begun to fall. No, you will not dance tonight." She rapped the shepherdess hook against the floor for emphasis, then exited the dressing room. Alexandra choked back a scream. It was a poor reason to keep her from the stage, when she could simply have changed costumes. Thus was the absolute tyranny of a costume mistress. With one dress, Madame could make or break a career. In fact, as Alexandra was learning, she could even prevent it from beginning at all.

"Cheer up, *ma cher*," sneered Marie-Louise. "At least

dancing isn't contingent upon your mastery of the French language. Then you would truly be out of luck."

"*Merde*, Marie-Louise," Alexandra said, offering the backstage colloquialism for "good luck," with a sweet smile. It also meant "shit." Marie-Louise narrowed her eyes. She knew Alexandra did not mean it in the congratulatory sense.

"I have learned another word," said Alexandra. "*Une chienne*." Marie-Louise gasped. That was French for "female dog," but there were no canines present. Marie-Louise moved as if to lunge at Alexandra, before deciding against it and quickly leaving the room. Alexandra lifted her chin. She had lost the battle, but she had gained a little ground.

"Isn't it marvelous how quickly I'm picking up the language?" Alexandra asked the room, purposefully speaking in English, so it didn't even matter if anyone understood her. The dancers were suddenly very preoccupied with powdering their noses and pulling up their tights, refusing to look her way in the mirror that stretched across the room.

Alexandra glanced down at her own costume, the deep red layers of her knee-length skirt, the front-hooks hidden beneath the beading of her corset. The indignity of being dressed to dance without being allowed to perform was like salt on a wound. It showed she had been foolish enough to hope. Alexandra cringed at her own naïveté. Everyone had seen her warm up, all the while knowing Madame wouldn't let her appear onstage tonight. Alexandra looked around the room. They all knew what she had not let herself even think: there was no way Madame would ever allow her to perform, not when Alexandra had railroaded her way into this world, barging past Monsieur's protests, fighting her way into the cast like a half-bit brawler. In this world, a performer earned her way onstage through a delicate dance of politics, bribes, and nuance. Alexandra had practically used brute force. A typical brash American, Alexandra had thought that once she was in the door, if she used enough butter, she could slide right into home. Not in Europe, not even in Monte Carlo. They would never forget her bullish entrance. For a place that promised a plethora of carefree hedonism, one could still be crushed under a hierarchy of rules.

Alexandra sighed and slipped her hand into her jar of hairpins, thinking she might as well use this time to practice the complicated coif preferred by the other chorus girls. Her hand stopped short when her fingers met something sticky. She lifted her hand to her nose. Honey. They had drowned her hairpins in honey. She had been doomed before she had even begun.

Alexandra could feel every pair of eyes in the dressing room watching her. If she weren't wearing her boots, she could guarantee she would have found broken glass in the toes of her ballet shoes. She tugged her dressing gown across her bodice and felt every bit the fool they thought her to be.

Her face grew warm and tears pricked the back of her eyes. It wasn't her fault she was new to Monaco, or that she had a Louisiana lilt to her broken French, or that she danced with a gusto Europe had never seen. Still, they blamed her for it, for her brashness, for her eagerness, for being simply different.

The assistant stage manager leaned into the dressing room, pushing his spectacles up onto his nose. "Cinque minutes, cinque minutes," he called.

"Merci, cinque minutes," echoed the room.

Alexandra couldn't bear to sit through another evening's performances, squishing herself against the walls while everyone else rushed through the costume changes and act breaks, shining with hard-earned sweat and adulation. She couldn't bear the sneers or, worse, the sideways pitying glances. She certainly couldn't bear to have anyone watch her cry because she had gotten a little honey on her fingers. She had to prove that they couldn't get the better of her.

She stood on her chair, leaned over the girls next to her, fumbling on the shelf above. She triumphantly grasped the bottle of wine she knew they hid there to help soothe nerves before a show or settle the post-performance rush. In full view of the entire dressing room, she yanked the cork from the bottle with her teeth, spit it onto the floor, and drank a large mouthful. She sputtered, then wiped her lips with the back of her hand. With a grand flourish of her arms, she whooped like a banshee before leaping from the chair and running from the room.

She stumbled over the ropes and sandbags lining the wings, ducked under flying scenery, and rushed down stairs and through halls, finally pushing her way out of the back-stage door into the fresh air and dark alley. The day was cooling into twilight, and the Mediterranean Sea glittered in the setting sun.

"Ladies and gentlemen," she shouted to no one in particular. "This evening's performance has been moved...to the beach!"

No one followed her, but Alexandra ran all the same.

ALEXANDRA CHARGED TOWARD THE BEACH, away from the glittering lights of the casino and the opera house. She didn't care that her costume would probably be ruined as she scuttled over rocks toward the emptiest part of the beach, away from the quay. *I would like to see Madame scold me*, she thought, defiantly.

The warm breeze of the Mediterranean blew against Alexandra's cheeks, meeting her tears. It was almost insulting; a cold breeze would have been more comforting.

Alexandra took a swig from the bottle of wine. *My only friend, ma chère amie,* she thought.

If the other dancers persisted in sabotaging her with their wide arsenal of petty show business tricks, Alexandra knew she would never make it onstage. She had to find a way to be accepted by them. If they accepted her, then Madame would accept her. She had only enough money for one more week at the dancers' boarding house, if she gave up eating now. If she didn't get paid, she'd have to take up residence elsewhere, perhaps on this very beach. Alexandra lifted her arm to watch the fringe of her dressing gown catch in the wind. Would her dressing gown be a sufficient shelter? She hoped never to find out.

Alexandra certainly didn't have the means to return to New Orleans, and she had no family waiting there. No family. That was a lump Alexandra still couldn't swallow. She took another gulp from the bottle, hoping that the lump, and the fear gripping her stomach, would melt away in a lovely burgundy tide.

Yes, if she couldn't turn things around soon, she would have to live on the beach. *Maybe I will turn into a mermaid,* Alexandra thought. That made her giggle. *La Sirène de Monte Carlo.* If she could sell herself as dancing mermaid, she could *sauté* her way out of the chorus and into a solo act, which was far more lucrative, both onstage and off.

Alexandra continued to pick her way over the rocks until she met the sand, which was cooling as the day set into twilight. She sat upon a rock to unlace her ankle-high boots and pull off her stockings. The delicate fabric of her wide calf-length skirt snagged on the rock. The straps of her beaded bodice fell around her shoulders. She looked every bit like the runaway she was.

Holding her shoes and stockings in one hand and the half-empty bottle of wine in the other, Alexandra picked her way along the beach, rounding the bend to the small cove she liked best. It was removed from the rest of beach and from prying eyes. Not that anyone would be looking for her. Everyone she knew here was already onstage.

There was one person who *should* be looking for her, but he never would.

Pierre. Whenever she thought his name, their affair felt like something that had happened a century ago. He had brought her to Monaco, seducing her heart and body with promises of love and adventure. After her parents' tragic carriage accident and the discovery that her inheritance would be needed to pay her parents' debts, it had been so easy to fall into Pierre's soft, soothing, deceptive hands. She had spent the entire voyage to the Mediterranean in a haze of lust and adoration, but soon after Monaco had appeared on the horizon, Pierre had vanished from her life. He'd taken her mother's necklace, a heavy length of pearls, the one thing she had hid from the creditors, and left her with only the clothes on her back and a steely resolve to survive. Not knowing what to do without her lover, and with the taste of adventure still on her lips, she had marched straight toward the most daring structure in her sightline, the Opéra de Monte Carlo. For a woman without means, abandoned on a foreign shore, her options were limited to drudgery, prostitution, or dancing. Alexandra had chosen dancing. If she was going to be destitute, she might as well be glamorous.

Except her current state was much less glamorous than she had hoped, even with her dancer's costume winking in the twilight.

Alexandra watched the waves lap the shore. It was peaceful here, as the first stars began their nightly promenade across the sky. The sky had faded from lavender to violet, and the full moon was already in sight. It would be a bright night.

Alexandra sighed. *What are we going to do?*

Since she had lost her family, she had come to think of the different parts of herself as a roving band of misfits, clunking along, somehow managing to muddle through, despite differing opinions and no clear driver. Spirit, mind, body, and heart; a family of four hitching on a single vessel, determined to survive, intact and together.

Oh, Alexandra's heart. Her treacherous heart. Always leading her to adventure. It lived wide open and singing, thrumming joyfully while it leapt into carriages and boats— or, even better, into the arms of a dark-eyed devil. Her dumb heart never considered the consequences; it simply launched itself bravely into each new adventure. Or misadventure, as was often the case. The more her heart was hurt, the more resolute it seemed to become. It insisted on being open to the world. *Come what may!*

So it was left to her brain to navigate the thorns and forests of wherever her heart had flung her. And this time her brain was fresh out of ideas. Over the past few weeks, since landing in Monaco, whenever Alexandra asked her brain what they should do, it shrugged silently and whispered a single response, *Come what may.*

"You're no help!" she said out loud, taking a long, defiant swig of the bottle. Her heart was no help, her brain was out of commission…what was left? Her body. What did her body think she should do? Her body, as always, wanted to move.

Alexandra took yet another drink from the bottle before anchoring it in the sand. The moon could act as spotlight. Alexandra planted her feet firmly in the sand. They could stop her from dancing before an audience, but they couldn't stop her from dancing before the waves.

Humming a melody all her own and using the beat of the waves as a percussive guide, Alexandra launched into her own dance solo. Raised near the music halls of New Orleans, her style was a mixture of the can-can she'd grown up with, an Irish jig she'd witnessed on the boat, and something else completely her own. Hers was the dance of a woman alone in the world, yet still determined to triumph. A woman who had been loved by her parents, her only family, who had buried them too soon, and then who had cast herself into the world, hoping for a soft place to land. The most forgiving place she had found was this beach. She had been enraptured by the warm climate, azure coastline, and the gritty glamour of a burgeoning opera house and casino. Monte Carlo aspired to opulence but wasn't yet sure it could attain it. It might sink as easily as it might rise. She felt kinship with this place that was uncertain of the grandeur of its own destiny. Monte Carlo, like her, aimed to be doing more than just fine.

The moon rose as Alexandra danced. Her toes flirted with the water's edge, flinging salt water onto her calves, drenching the edge of her skirt. She pulled her skirt higher, scandalously revealing her strong thighs. What did it matter? No one would watch her dance tonight. She could do as she liked. Alexandra's hair shook completely loose of its last pin, sending her dark curls tumbling over her shoulders. She was spectacularly disheveled, yet it was the best she had felt in weeks.

Alexandra stomped and splashed in the edges of the water, kicking her legs high, throwing her head back. She spun, circling her head so that her hair whipped about her neck and face. From somewhere, a warm breeze came upon her, crawling up her breasts and lifting her hair off her neck. She swept her hands along her body following that breeze, catching her hair in her hands, flinging her arms open to welcome the wind.

A flash of light from the water caught the corner of her vision. She stopped to look, expecting to see a dim lantern on small vessel. The waves dipped and surged, and there was nothing. Then it was there again—another flash, golden, not firelit but iridescent, glinting off the water.

The darkening sky could not illuminate what the waves obscured, and yet Alexandra knew something was out there. Or someone. That same warm breeze blew against her skin, bringing the tangy scent of salt water and something else to her. Was it...a man? *Ridiculous*, she thought. *There is no man out there.* Yet she could feel she was being watched...and she liked it.

Alexandra changed the motion of her dancing, stretching one leg out before her to trace a long circle in the water. A circle that made its way up her leg to her hips where it transformed into a figure eight, unleashing a sensual sway that overtook her entire body. A wave surged up to her, splashing against her thighs. *Is this how Delilah frolicked in the bath for Samson?* She felt like Jezebel, the Queen of Sheba, and a siren high on her own dangerous beauty all at once. She felt wanton, for sure, but there was also great power to the feeling. This was a new dance for her—a dance that could lead the viewer along and then stop him when she had him right where wanted him.

She cast her glance back to the water, continuing to circle her hips, afraid that if she stopped, this mystery witness would retreat. Who was watching her?

The mere idea of being watched while she moved like this excited her. Alexandra felt dampness between her legs, and it wasn't a splash of sea water. The gaze from the water stuck to her like a magnet, traveling from her ankles to her belly. But who would dare look at her like this, and who could remain hidden for so long?

3

A CHANCE ENCOUNTER

When he'd raced to the surface, Triton had been thinking solely about destruction and revenge. He'd been focused on hunting down the miscreant of a prince who had dared to dally with his youngest daughter and her tender heart. Triton had broken through the surface, scanning the coast for a good place to come ashore, a place that would bring him close to where he might hunt down this prince. It wasn't until he had surfaced that he realized he had no idea *which* prince had interfered with his daughter, nor any idea of where he might live. The details of human land boundaries meant nothing to him, but no matter, he would scent out where his daughter had been, search every bit of coastline if need be. All for the pleasure of wringing that mortal's neck, perhaps impaling him on his trident while the man screamed.

Keeping himself stealthily submerged, Triton had scouted the rocky shoreline. There were too many ships in the quay for him to come ashore there; ships meant sailors, and the only sailors Triton liked were the ones he found crushed under shipwrecks on the ocean floor. Finally, he found a sweet little cove around the bend from the bay.

He swam toward the cove, stopping abruptly when he saw her on the beach. His past had made him leery of beautiful maidens in secret coves. Yet something about this maiden was different. He swam closer for a better look. She was beguiling, certainly, but was she also a threat?

She had no lantern, but his keen vision and the faint dusk had illuminated everything he needed to see. The deep scarlet of her dress, her dark, glossy hair and ruby lips, the summoning motions of her body. He had never seen a human move like that. Mostly he found mortals clumsy, heavy-limbed, and awkward. Being bi-pedal made them lumber along, whereas merfolk could soar. But this mortal, she was a water storm unto herself. As she undulated and writhed, she told a story, a story he recognized because it was exactly the way he had felt, racing to the surface just now. It was a story of rage, and unacknowledged power, a story of being denied, and a story of twisting that denial into something more powerful—the desire to annihilate and avenge. His own body could not move as she did, but his heart and blood knew that cadence all the same. Yes, she was a threat, but not to him.

Triton's nostrils flared as a surge of lust overcame him. He breathed deeply, his heart pounding with desire. Although he tried to quell the feeling, he was always surprised by the seduction of the salt air. It brought to him sensations and information that were delivered very differently underwater. Underwater, if a female desired him, he might notice it as the water drifted past him. But here, the breeze delivered to him the scent of a passionate woman, and once it arrived, he could not bear to release it.

Triton clenched his fist around his trident. Contact between humans and merfolk was forbidden. Hadn't he just surfaced to bring retribution for a breach of this very ordinance?

Triton turned to leave but gave one last glance back to the beach. The dancer had stopped, her gaze focused on the water. She knew he was there. Triton swallowed. Would she run? Would she scream? Would she come closer? Or would she pretend he didn't even exist? Humans were adept at that, ignoring any realities of the world that didn't suit them.

The dancer did none of these. Instead, she did something Triton had not expected. The merest hint of a smile touched her lips as she extended her leg and swiveled her hips, beginning a new chain of erotic movement.

Triton's heart leapt to his throat. She was no longer dancing for herself. She was dancing for him. He felt himself harden, and his breath catch. This new dance invited his gaze and offered a world of wonders to gaze upon: dark hair that whipped in the breeze; full, round breasts set high above a broad waist that tapered into even more ample hips. Triton catalogued the treasures of her body one by one, like seashells collected along the shore. He felt the way he had when he had swum upon his first sea-mountain, awed by the scope of its peaks and valleys, yearning to grip his fingers into its holds.

"Fish-rot and fire," Triton swore under his breath. This human was taunting him with her wide thighs that begged to have teeth sunk into them. Worse, it was working.

The right thing to do would be to leave. The right thing to do would be to sink back under the waves and find a new cove. After all, he was here for revenge, not for recreation. But then that damned puckish breeze came to him again, bringing the scent of her arousal, the smell of her hair and skin. Triton wanted her, no matter what his rules decreed. And when the King of the Sea wanted something, he got it.

There were two ways to work out rage, he reasoned to

himself. The first was violence, the second was coupling. Surely he could abandon, at least temporarily, his plan to murder that idiot prince. Instead, he could annihilate himself upon the body of a woman.

WHAT HAD BEEN a single glow point was now a five-pointed gleaming object. A crown? It couldn't be. She kept circling her hips, hoping their magic would hold her audience. She needed to see just what was out there. What was watching her? Or *who*? A fire lit in her belly at the thrill of discovering this mystery man, for although she could not see him, somehow she knew the presence was male. This intuition was proven by how her desire pooled lower down, taunting her in the same way that her dance was taunting this unknown man.

As if her arousal were a stage cue, her mystery audience member surged into view, like a volcano upon the horizon. The gleaming five-pointed object was indeed a crown, set atop a crest of rich silver hair that blended into a long, thick beard. Alexandra gasped—first that there was indeed a man in the water, and second at the realization that silver hair could be so overwhelmingly virile. The ends of his beard lay against a broad, muscled chest and shoulders that tapered into a strong waist that would be like wrapping her legs around a cannon. The vee of it descended into something slicker, shimmering, solid…a tail? As he drew closer, two heavily muscled arms emerged from the water, one of which held a glowing trident that shed more light on his magnificent form.

Oh my gravy, I have conjured a sea god, thought Alexandra. *Either I am an enchantress, or this is a dream.* A wonderful, hazy, moonlit dream that she hoped she would not wake up from before she was able to see all of him. Feel all of him.

The sea god moved toward her through the waves, which parted for him and created an iridescent golden path that led straight to her. In the space between the rise and dip of a wave, his tail vanished to reveal two thick, strong thighs... and a manhood that was most definitely divine.

Alexandra flushed. She shouldn't look so boldly upon a deity, but how could she not? The sea god stalked through the surf with the grace and purpose of a panther. His gaze pinned her to the spot. She wondered if she should be afraid, but she was not. She was curious about him, sure, but the flutters deep within her told her it was more than that. Something in her beckoned to him, and he was merely answering the call.

The sea god stood a few feet from her, ankle deep in the water, his trident planted firmly in the sand. He crossed his arms, the thick ropes of his biceps framing the darkness of his nipples. Alexandra thought she would like to place her cheek against his chest, perhaps even be forced to hold her face there while the rest of her body did...other things. Alexandra swallowed hard, unable to blink, or move, or think while the sea god regarded her so intently.

It seemed they were at an impasse, each transfixed by the other, neither wanting to break the spell. The breeze fluttered through the sea god's silver mane and beard, sending a sensual shiver down Alexandra's spine. If his brilliant hair were a silver mirror, all she would see reflected would be the sparking flames of her growing desire. He lifted his chin slightly, as if he could smell her burgeoning arousal. The biggest point of his crown gleamed brighter. Message received... and accepted.

The gleaming of his crown brought Alexandra to her senses. Although she had little experience with royalty, and even less experience with devastatingly handsome demi-gods who rose from the sea on full-moon nights, she did know some sort of greeting was in order. Alexandra crossed one ankle behind the other and dipped into what she hoped was a sufficiently low curtsy.

The sea god circled her, coming close enough that she could smell him, all salt air, heat, and power. That warm wind brushed against her skin again, and she guessed he could control the elements if he wanted to. He stopped before her, his muscled calves consuming her line of vision.

"Rise," he ordered her, his voice gravelly and low. She obeyed, drawing herself up slowly so she could savor the rewarding view of his legs, his thighs, and the thick length of him. Her eyes traveled further up his torso, past the sculpted hardness of his abdomen and right into his bright blue eyes. Once, on a clear day on the ship to Monaco, Alexandra had seen a sea so calm that it was more window than ocean. That is what it was like looking into the sea god's eyes, a bright refraction resting atop a deeper mystery.

What does one say to a sea god, or should I wait for him to speak again?

The sea god raked his eyes over her body, taking as much time to soak her in as she had taken with him. He lingered over the bend of her waist, the arch of breasts as her breath came, heavy now, her heart thundering faster with each second of his gaze. He reached a hand out to catch one of her curls, then laid it softly back on her shoulder.

Was this madness? Magic? Witchcraft? Delirium? Minutes ago, she had been lower than scum at the Opéra de Monte Carlo. Now before her stood a god of the sea, naked, with legs where she had just seen a tail, looking at her as if she were a feast hastily readied for a starving king. Alexandra's skin tingled, her nerves trilling like nightingales. What should she do? Scream, run, faint?

What do we do? What do we do? She scanned through her mind, heart, and spirit, each of which was paralyzed. All that was left to guide her was her body. Her body, which prickled with goosebumps and churned with longing. Her body saw the tsunami of desire in the sea god's eyes and said, *Let me drown.*

It was settled then. Her body had set the course. All Alexandra had to do was surrender.

"Do you belong to anyone?" he asked.

"No," she whispered.

"Good," he said, "because tonight, you belong to the King of the Sea."

Alexandra nodded, and that was all the invitation the sea god needed.

4

WHEN LAND MEETS SEA

*T*riton's possessive words still hung in the air. He was ready to claim her, but would she accept? Lust gathered deep in his belly. This had not been his plan to begin with, but by Poseidon was it his plan now.

He anchored his trident in the wet sand beside her. She was not afraid to meet his gaze, although she appeared to have some difficulty speaking. Triton couldn't blame her. At this moment, he was having trouble doing anything but desiring her.

Triton bent his head, his lips nearly touching hers. "Would you like to be claimed by me?" he asked. He kept his tone light so she would know that she could refuse. Although it would torture him, he would leave her be if she wished it.

A sly grin spread across her face as she realized her position of power. She hesitated, bringing her face infinitesimally closer to his, just to draw out her reply. Only the merest sliver of wind could have fit between them now. Finally, she spoke. "Yes."

Triton cupped her face in his wide, strong hands. "As you wish," he said, bending his head to take her lips.

She met him halfway, taking his mouth as enthusiastically as he did hers. Triton sucked and pulled on her lips, eliciting a soft sigh from her, before diving in with his tongue. He kept his kiss firm, insistent, but patient, letting her know that there was much more to come, and he would take his time getting there.

She wound her arms around his neck, twisted her hands into his hair, and pressed herself against his chest. Her kiss was as insistent. The tantalizing movements of her mouth egged him on, increasing the pleasure of his pursuit. This was no shy tide fish, no swooning, useless mortal maiden. For the first time in centuries, Triton thought he might have met a mortal who could hold her own. He felt an odd tug of emotion adjacent to his desire. Was it respect? Triton shoved that thought to the back of his mind. He'd think about that later, when he was back on his throne, where everything made sense, not above the surface, where all was topsy-turvy and a mortal woman could enchant a god and a king.

Triton dragged his knuckles down her neck, along the soft skin of her shoulders, landing on the side of her breast. He drew the back of his hand along its curve, tracing a languid semicircle. She shuddered and leaned further into him. She felt flushed against him, like a rock warmed in the sun. His lips continued their exploration, moving to her earlobe and her neck, nibbling his way to her collarbone. He breathed in her scent—soap, sweat, and heightened arousal. It had been ages since he had been attracted to a human, but this whirling dervish had captivated him. He wanted to make her moan, make her undulate beneath him in the same way she had danced.

She broke off the kiss, breathy and wild-eyed. Triton placed a hand on the small of her back. "Is something wrong?"

"I must know one thing, before we continue," she said.

Triton pressed her to him. "Anything," he whispered. He'd give over any secret of the deep if he could keep kissing her.

"I must know…" She hesitated. "I must know if you plan to kill me, or capture me…eventually, I mean."

Triton cocked his head. It hadn't occurred to him, but he was also impressed that she had thought to ask. It was clever of her, considering how many legends ended with demi-gods dragging women into the underworld. Oddly, her wariness earned a sliver of his trust. He liked the reminder that she was risking something, too.

"I can assure you," Triton said, "that I had not planned on either."

The woman gave a demure smile. "Good," she said, "because I am alone in the world, and it would be very aggravating to have to avenge my death all by myself."

Triton laughed, the sound raw and unusual to his ears. How long had it been since he had laughed? Had a mortal ever made him laugh? And what did she mean that she was truly alone in the world?

Triton had felt lonesome after his queen had died, and he'd mourned her deeply, but he had never felt *alone*. He could not imagine the feeling, given his many children, his court, and the pantheon of deities in his acquaintance.

He felt almost moved to pity her, yet the jut of her chin reminded him of a warrior. She'd push him out of the way if she tried to protect her, so it was best to stand beside her. Or lie beneath her. Triton suddenly remembered exactly why he had always liked the pluckiest fish best. He was surprised to find his heart warm to a human along with his body.

"I swear to you," he said, "that only good will come to you by my hands."

To illustrate his point, Triton moved his hands to her rump, grasping each cheek so he could press himself against her most sensitive parts while he nipped and licked at the edges of her bodice. She tightened her hands in his hair, urging him to go on. His hard length pressed against her belly, seeking her heat. He bent his head, tugged at the edges of her bodice with his teeth until with one savage whip of his head, he wrenched the fabric off one breast.

Her nipple peaked, bared to the night. He set his mouth on it, sucking and licking, his other hand caressing her breast, encouraged by her low moans. While Triton found most human clothing ridiculous, he supposed he now agreed that these complicated bodices made for a fantastic reveal of flesh.

Triton's hand drew along her thigh, bringing her leg to wrap against his waist so he could better angle himself as she ground against him. Her hands ran frantically across his shoulders, biceps, and upper back. He felt her nails dig into him as he teased her nipple and rubbed against her core. She moaned into his ear, her arousal blooming, engulfing each of his senses. Triton reveled in the warmth of her, the way she burned hot against his cooler chest, reminding him of the singular pleasure of lounging on a rock warmed by the sun. It was a respite for a king who had grown accustomed to ignoring the smaller pleasures of life.

Triton took her mouth again. She dragged her hands across his sculpted abdomen, scratching her nails against him. He growled as her hands encased his hardness. Without hesitation, she gripped the underside of his length, stroking upward to the head, twisting her hand around the tip on the downward stroke. He gasped as she stroked him, firmly and with purpose, building his pleasure with near-malicious precision. He felt his cock swelling larger and larger. As a lover, she was rare find. Through a blur of breath and desire, he wondered if she was indeed human. Surely she had to be part enchantress.

Triton opened his eyes. He needed to see what other

delights this treasure had to offer. His large hands cupped and massaged her breasts firmly, making her throw her head back. He tweaked her covered nipple through the fabric, bringing a grin to her face. So she liked it a little rough, he mused. He gripped the center of her bodice, flexed his biceps, and prepared to rip it straight through the middle.

"Wait!" She gasped. "It hooks in the front!" He paused, considering whether his own delight in tearing her garment from her body would outweigh her displeasure at him doing so.

She seemed to read his mind. "I'm sure you could rip through whalebone, but it isn't necessary." She moved his hands back to her waist. "Here, I'll show you."

She stepped back with a saucy wink and, ever so slowly, began to undo her bodice, hook by hook. By Poseidon, Triton had felt more patience waiting twelve hours for a tide to come in. He felt each pop of the hook thrum through his body. He was caught in a delicious eternity, trapped between the gratification of the reveal of each inch of her flesh and the exquisite torment of not being allowed to hurry it along. How strange it was that he spent his life with frequent views of the female torso and yet the moment he encountered one that was covered up, he felt as if he might die if he could not gaze upon her lovely breasts.

Finally—finally—she reached the last hook, pushing her breasts toward him as her bodice fell open. She gathered the straps from her shoulders and in one swift movement pushed the garment off her body. One last tug on the skirt and she was free, bared to him in the moonlight. Her breasts hung, heavy and full, and he thought that if moon vanished forever, he would not miss it for he would spend his life worshipping her perfect orbs instead.

She stepped into his waiting arms so he could nuzzle and caress her. What had he been thinking, preventing contact with the human world? *Humans*, he thought as he dropped kisses on her breasts, *are fantastic*.

There was, however, one more obstacle in Triton's path.

He glowered at the thin silk of her undergarments, which covered her from her navel to the tops of her thighs. She giggled at the ferociousness of his expression. "I'll help you find your way around this," she said.

She ran her fingers down his cheeks to thread her hands in his beard, stroking the underside of his chin with her fingertips. Standing on her tiptoes, she kissed him softly. "First, you'll have to meet face to face."

She tugged on his beard, drawing him down until he was on his knees. Triton's eyes flared. This human was forcing him to kneel, and judging from the tightness of his balls, he liked it. Her hand pressed against the back of his head, drawing him close until his lips were just against her center.

Triton breathed her in. Here was the source of her arousal, the same scent that had called him out of the water. It was spicy, heady, intoxicating, and completely her. She nudged against him, impatient, but he had a few ideas of his own. With the lightest touch, he ran his hands from her ankles to her calves, reveling in the forbidden delight of caressing a pair of human legs. These were the very symbol of his enemy, which is perhaps why he found them so enticing. It helped that this pair was well developed and long, but he was attracted to them because he had seen them used to express something. Her legs were powerful and mystical, where most were utilitarian. He roamed his hands over her rump, enjoying the heft and heat of her. In the water, a body could feel slippery, ephemeral. Here was something solid, warm, and abundant, something he could hold onto, something he could cling to. He could wreck himself again and again upon her shore, and she would still be there, unharmed and welcoming.

Triton spread his hands along the backs of her wide, lush thighs and returned to the pleasures spread before him. He set his mouth against the silk of her undergarments, letting his hot breath penetrate them before he licked her though the fabric. His tongue twirled against her, echoing the movements he had seen her make on the beach. She ground against his mouth, panting and moaning as his tongue dipped between her folds, using the fabric to as an extra tool of delicious torture. He traced a finger along the edge of her undergarment, hooking his finger to meet inside where his mouth lay above. While his tongue licked her tight, hot bud, his knuckle dragged across her folds, finally slipping inside of her. She was hot, wet, moving against him, hungry for more, needing more of him, but he would only give it to her when he was good and ready. When she could take the agony no longer, she used her own hands to tug down her undergarments, stepping out of them while he kept his mouth on her. Now she was completely bare, freed of everything from the human world, ready to be claimed by him. An offering to the powers of the sea. She grasped the ends of his mustache and anchored his mouth to her, prepared to steer him right to the edge of her pleasure.

Triton slipped his tongue deep inside her, gripping her waist to thrust her against his face. Her juices dripped over his mouth and beard, filling him with her scent, driving him wilder. He threw her leg over his shoulder, thrusting two fingers in her, rolling her swollen pearl between his lips. Her hands gripped the points of his crown, helping his rhythm, bringing her to higher and higher heights. Triton swirled his fingers inside of her until he felt her squeeze around him and shatter with her climax. Her hips pumped against his face, she rode out the waves of her orgasm with the five points of his crown tight against the luscious rolls of her belly. Her throbbing subsided, and he removed his fingers, dropping tender kisses in the crease of her thigh.

Her hands on his head, she brought him back to her face, kissing him, tasting herself on him, trembling in his arms.

"I must know one thing," he murmured, smiling as he echoed her earlier words. "Before we continue."

She returned his playful grin. "Anything," she whispered.

"Tell me your name."

"Why?" she asked.

"So that I may say it when I take you."

She smiled against his lips, kissing him deeply.

"Alexandra. You may call me Alexandra."

Gripping Alexandra, his Alexandra, around the waist with one arm, he grabbed his trident with other, circling the tips over the sand. A thin, shimmering coverlet settled over the sand, a bed made of light. Triton lowered her to the ground, taking his time to fan her hair around her face. His fingers made gentle trails along her body, from head to toe, lingering on the tips of her breasts, the curves of her waist, watching her sigh and writhe in response to his touch. He rolled her to her side, sitting back on his heels to enjoy the sight of her. He knew now why human mythology cast hill ranges as the form of sleeping goddesses. She was all broad peaks and rolling hills, the picture of verdant abundance, redolent with the kind of desire that promised prosperity of every manner. If he were a mere man, he would have bowed before her, knowing his unworthiness. As the King of the Sea, he knew there was only one way to properly worship her.

Triton lay beside her, drew her leg around his waist. Grasping his length in one hand, he rubbed the head of his length against her slit. He could feel her slickness, softer and sweeter than an oyster shell. Alexandra nudged her hips toward him, the best encouragement he knew.

"Alexandra," he murmured against her lips. He kissed her softly and then pushed the full length of himself inside of her. They moaned together. This was heaven; this was bliss. The moon shone high in the sky, and everything was right.

Triton rolled onto his back so Alexandra could sit astride him. Together, they found a rhythm that suited them both. He ran his hands up her waist, cupping her breasts as she bounced above him. He let her set the pace, feeling her begin to clench and throb around him. Her eyes were closed, her hands braced against his chest, her breath coming heavier.

She paused, opening her eyes, gazing down at him. "What do I call you?" she asked, smiling.

"Why?" he asked, smiling back.

She gripped his wrists, placed his hands above his head, and held them there. Triton paused. Was this human really daring to pin down a king? Would he allow it?

She shifted the rhythm of her hips, bearing down to grip him, bringing him deeper inside of her. He threw his head back and moaned. Yes, he would allow it. He would allow it very, very much.

"Tell me so I can cry your name," Alexandra demanded.

"Triton," he gasped. "But you will call me, 'My lord.'"

Alexandra laughed at his moment of sternness. "My lord," she said and moved faster against him. She rode him with intensity. Her breasts swung in his face, and he made a game of trying to catch her nipple with his lips. Her breath was hot, and her body grew slick as she moved faster and faster. He grew harder, heat gathering his belly, his balls tightening. Alexandra rode him harder, her body a whipping wave racing toward a shore break. They were suspended in time, both focused only on chasing their release, until Alexandra gave a small cry, her body surging over him, the ripples of her climax reverberating through him as well.

She fell against his chest, soft and vulnerable, and something inside of Triton broke. He didn't want to be filled with rage. He didn't want to use her body just so he could spill forth his feelings with his seed. He wanted to protect her, to match himself to her splendor. He wanted to watch her dance, both on the beach and over him. He wanted to celebrate her with his body, offer her a piece of his heart to keep, a piece of his heart that ruled nothing and no one but was kept because she liked it and him. He wanted to give a part of himself to her, so he could watch her revel in it. He wanted to be a sea god worthy of this land goddess.

The movements of her body had changed him. In the way a wave shapes a sea cliff, his armor had been eroded. He had come to this beach with something burning in him, and now it had washed away forever. While in the white flame of his climax, he knew he was glad to be rid of it, whatever it had been. His hands wrapped around Alexandra's waist, and after one final thrust, Triton withdrew, the white foam waves of his climax breaking on her stomach.

"Alexandra," he said, hips bucking, salt tears on his cheeks. "Alexandra."

Off the coast, a flash of lightning struck the ocean. The King of the Sea had been satisfied.

5

A PASSIONATE TIDE

*A*lexandra slid to the ground beside Triton, breath heaving, heart pounding, a marvelous glow filling her from head to toe. Had she really just been ravished by a sea king? And, indeed, had she herself just ravished the sea king? Maiden ravishing happened in myths, but nowhere in the story of Leda and the Swan had it said that Leda grabbed Zeus's beard until he set his mouth on center of her femininity. She was fairly certain that legend had also not mentioned Leda pinning Zeus's hands above his head while she rode him right toward a spectacular climax.

Alexandra cringed inwardly. She had hardly asked him who he was or where exactly he came from! She had just surrendered to him immediately, expending her fury at Madame on him. Perhaps it was best, though. Most legends counseled against refusing the gods, and she only knew the vaguest details about the legends of the sea deity known as Triton. Besides, she had wanted him. From the first moment she had felt his gaze upon her from the water, she had wanted him. When he had stalked straight to her and declared his intent to have her, she had been relieved and thrilled. She would have had no idea how to make herself enticing to a sea king. Alexandra remembered that he had spilled himself on her stomach. A quick brush of her hand revealed that she was not wet. Rather, all she felt a thin veil of salt clinging to her skin. How curious.

Alexandra realized her eyes were still closed. Should she open them? Would he still be there if she did? Most likely, he would be gone. She felt a coldness in her stomach. She would be left again, alone, friendless and on the edge of poverty. How could she expect a lover who had emerged from the sea to remain on the land? If she opened her eyes, she was sure he would vanish, as mysteriously as he had arrived. Yet the throbbing between her legs told her that she hoped he would still be there.

Alexandra steeled herself and decided to meet reality. She fluttered her eyes open slowly, casting a careful glance to the side. Triton was indeed still beside her. What's more, he was turned toward her, his head propped on an elbow, gazing at her with an unreadable expression. Since he had already responded so well to her boldness, Alexandra resolved to continue in that vein. She mimicked his pose and met his gaze. Neither of them spoke. Both of their chests still heaved with the aftereffects of lovemaking.

Finally, Triton broke their staring contest. "You are a curious human."

Alexandra laughed, which made Triton laugh, which made Alexandra laugh more. "You're a curious...you're a curious...who are you?" asked Alexandra as her giggles subsided.

Triton smiled and traced a large thumb over her hip. "I am Triton, King of the Sea."

Alexandra noted the gold cuffs around his wrists and stroked her thumb over their coolness, encouraging Triton's caresses. "And what brought you here tonight, Triton, King of the Sea?" she asked.

He frowned slightly, and Alexandra caught a glimpse of the power that lay within him. "I was looking for something."

"Did you find it?"

"In a way." He caught her hand and brought her fingers to his lips. Alexandra felt her nerves race again at his kiss.

"I enjoyed your dancing," he said.

Alexandra blushed. "No one was supposed to be watching that."

"You were angry," Triton observed.

Alexandra cast a glance in the direction of the casino. "Yes, I was."

"Why?" Triton asked, his eyes beginning to glow hot. Alexandra had a feeling that if she told him the location of Madame's bed, he might stalk right up there and smother her in her sleep.

"I dance for the opera house." She gestured to the glittering lights in the distance.

"Others see you dance?" He seemed alarmed, hurt even, that her private seduction might have been a mimicry of a public performance.

"No, no," Alexandra rushed to soothe him. "You are the first to see me dance...in that way. That was new. At first I did it for me, but when I felt you watching, it became a dance for you." She wanted him to know he was special, that he had witnessed something original in her.

He looked pleased, almost puffed up, to have been her muse. "You must be very, very popular. If I could look at you every night, I would never let you leave the room." Alexandra was touched by the reverence in his voice.

"Unfortunately, it's quite the opposite." She laughed, imagining Marie-Louise's face if she broke into rehearsal with that particular frenzy that Triton had witnessed. "That's the problem. They won't let me dance."

"Why not?" Triton frowned.

"It's hard to say, exactly. They think I am too bold, or out of place. They don't want me to dance with them. And if they won't let me dance eventually, I can't live."

Triton tensed, ready to fight. "Have you been bewitched?" He seemed concerned that her destiny could be tied to a curse, sentenced to death through dance.

Alexandra smiled. "No, nothing like that. I mean that if I can't dance, they won't pay me, and I won't have anything to eat. Or anywhere to go."

Alexandra wondered if it was strange to state her circumstances so bluntly to a stranger, especially one who likely had a chapter in an ancient text of mythology, but it didn't *feel* strange. It felt friendly. After all, they had already shared quite a bit of intimacy. Triton nodded at her answer, as if he understood, although as King of the Sea, he most likely always had somewhere to go.

Imagine that. Always being welcome. Being able to command your environment to welcome you.

"They are fools. Idiots. I could send a tidal wave to punish them," Triton offered, his hand reaching for his trident.

Alexandra quickly placed her hand on his forearm. "No!" She took the edge off her voice. "I mean, no, thank you. It's very kind of you to offer, but I would rather win them over than destroy them."

"You are not afraid of a challenge, then." Triton stroked the edges of his beard slowly. "That is good. That will serve you well."

The sight of Triton's strong hands in his soft beard stirred something in Alexandra. She threaded her fingers through it, scratching the underside of his chin. "No." Her voice became throaty. "I am not afraid of a challenge." It was rather soon to begin stirring up her passion again, but Alexandra thought she did not have time to waste. At any moment, he would disappear, like the salt flakes on her skin.

Triton made a rumbling sound of deep satisfaction and bent his head to kiss her. She wanted to meet his mouth eagerly but kept her lips soft, coy. Triton smiled against her lips, catching onto the game. He nibbled at her lips, catching and releasing her in languid intervals. He moved to kiss her jaw, take a brief nip at her earlobe, then nuzzle and suck her neck, just behind her ear—her favorite spot. Alexandra arched her chest to turn herself closer to him. Triton dragged his hands over her shoulders, down her back, clutching her to him while he trailed kisses down her body.

Triton lifted his head to trail his gaze down her body. With a flick of his wrist, his trident glowed brighter, bathing Alexandra like candlelight. "It is dark, and I want to see all of you," Triton said.

Alexandra's hips bucked in response. She knew she was lush in frame and plentiful in build. Sometimes she wondered if perhaps she was too lush, but Triton's gaze made her feel as if she could offer every inch she had, and he would still be starving for more. Alexandra stretched her legs alongside him, pointing her toes, elongating her figure so he had miles and miles to gaze upon. Triton grunted with satisfaction, moving swiftly to cover her with his large torso. His head bent to her nipple, careful that his crown avoided her face. His warm mouth teased her, the flicks of his tongue strumming her like a guitar. An obedient little instrument of pleasure, she moaned along with his attentions. Triton's hands ran over her stomach, her hips, her thighs, coaxing along the nerves that trilled up and down her body.

Alexandra dragged a toe up Triton's solid calves, feeling their smoothness. How could he feel so much like a man when she knew he had another form, a strong, slick form

LAURA LOVELY

that propelled him through his wide domain? Alexandra draped a thigh over Triton's hip, her body blossoming at the memory of how his rugged physique had felt gripped between her legs. She had the urge to know what the rest of him felt like, the part usually hidden beneath the water. She wanted to know what it would feel like to be taken by him in his true form, the one that reigned over the sea and every creature in it. This might be the only night in her life that she would ever be ravaged by a sea king, and she wanted to take full advantage of it.

Triton dragged his teeth over the curve of her breast, causing her gasp. She bent her head to his ear.

"Could we go to the water?" She breathed.

Triton lifted his head to meet her gaze, curious.

Alexandra bit her lip, not sure how to phrase what she wanted. "I want to know all of you...your other form. I want you to take me...in the water."

Triton's eyes darkened with pleasure. "It will be different," he warned. "It won't be anything like what we did before."

Alexandra's heart soared into her throat. All she could do was nod. *Yes, please. Show me that.*

Triton scooped her up in his arms and strode splashing into the water. Alexandra wrapped her arms around his neck, pressed her cheek to his chest, feeling his heartbeat thud in her ears. She felt protected, cherished even. She stretched into this moment of connection, knowing soon she would return to her real life, to her isolation. But for now, she could bask in the sensation of being carried, of being cared for.

Once they were waist high, his movements changed. His swagger morphed into a glide. His arms lowered so that Alexandra was submerged up to her neck. She shivered, and Triton held her closer.

Triton shifted her so that she faced him. "Wrap your legs around my waist," he said.

Alexandra crossed her legs behind Triton's back. Her heels brushed against his lower half, smooth and firm, like muscle wrapped in a thick layer of satin. In this position, her center was laid bare to him. She felt where the hard muscles of his abdomen met the silky flesh of his tail. Triton cupped her rump in his hands, flexing and gripping his fingers to mold her against him. With her most sensitive parts, she could feel exactly how the man in him met the animal of him. It was half cool, half warm against her, like a tongue manipulating melted ice. Beneath his tail, the male part of him was hidden—and, in its current state, partially stiff. She was reminded of knuckles under a silk glove, of what it was like to slide against a rigid thigh. She wondered if it too had transformed or merely retracted. But before she could wonder anything else, Triton's hands encouraged her to rub against him, to explore exactly how he fit together, how exactly he could please her in this form. Alexandra rocked against him while he swam leisurely, the water at her back sluicing a stream over her thighs, a bubbling hose that tickled at her most sensitive spot. Alexandra clenched as a shiver ran through her.

She half-opened her eyes. His iridescent trail followed them, golden sparks mixed with the moonlit water caps.

"Are you taking me far away?" she murmured. Would he take her to his underwater palace? *Could* he take her underwater? Although she could swim, she was not experienced in the water. She should have been nervous, but he made her feel safe. If anything had been proven in the past hour, it was that he was utterly devoted to the safety of her body.

"I'm taking you right where I want you," he answered. They veered toward a crop of rocks at the tip of the cove. Gently, Triton placed her back against a smooth rock, using his body weight to hold her in place. Alexandra looked down at her body, as if she had never seen it before. The water trickling over her shoulders and clavicle, her hair floating in the water, her breasts bobbing enticingly in the waves, perfect, like cream overflowing a silver cup. All of her bathed in a silver light, highlighted by the golden glow of Triton's crown. She felt a lump in her throat. She looked so beautiful. How had she never noticed it before?

Triton took one of her nipples in his lips. Alexandra tilted her head back.

I am a goddess. He has made me a goddess. I am made of the moon.

Alexandra ran her hands over his arms, the biceps that were so gargantuan they could only belong to an immortal king. She had seen statues of gods before but had attributed their giant scale to the power of myth. Now she knew those fountains and monuments to be accurate representations. These particular almighty biceps held her in place like a loving fortress, shelter, sanctuary, and strength all combined. She loved the way each wave brought him to her, over and over again. Alexandra dragged her hands down his back. She wanted to explore more of him, to know all that was possible in this form. Her hand met the slick hump of the top of his tail. She gave a tentative squeeze, delighted to find that felt just as firm and satisfying as his human behind. Triton nipped her breast with his teeth, urging her on. Alexandra moved her hand around his waist to the front, noting that his scales were sharper when she moved against the grain.

At his front, she slipped her hand between them. Here was more of the same firm muscle, but when she cupped her hand and kneaded her fingers, she felt a ridge harden more beneath her hands, his length still tucked away from view but ready for her. It felt like a secret only she could draw forth.

Triton pressed her harder against the rock. Alexandra's

outstretched hands grasped at the crevices, looking for purchase to leverage herself against Triton while he nipped and licked at her breasts. With a growl, Triton flipped Alexandra around. Her cheek scraped against the wet rock, Triton's lips on her back. Her fingers slipped, and she wondered how she would hold herself here. Triton surged above the water, quickly transferring his golden cuffs from his wrists to hers. The magic golden cuffs chained her to the rock, holding her both safely and seductively. She was splayed against the stone, her top half exposed to the salt air, her bottom half hidden in the water. Like Triton, she could have been anything from the waist down. This was the closest she might ever get to being a mermaid, bound to a rock by the sea king.

Alexandra's mind flitted to the story of Andromeda, chained as a sacrifice to the Kraken. The paintings depicted Andromeda twisting away, or languishing amongst the surf, prone, decorative, and desperate, an object waiting to be rescued. Alexandra felt like the exact opposite. The salt air blowing against her skin, her fingers flexing against the rock, the feel of the surf rising and falling against her, blind to what Triton had planned for her—all of it thrilled her. She felt powerful—Triton wanted *her*, and he wanted her *there*, like *this*, open to him and unable to see what was coming. In this scenario, she wanted more than anything to be devoured by this sea monster.

Triton moved her dripping hair over her shoulder, kissing his way down her back, pausing at her hips. She could feel his gaze, watching the waves play against the curves of her backside, revealing and hiding, revealing and hiding, a watery peep show.

"So beautiful," he whispered.

His hands massaged her hips, one diving around to her front, slipping a finger into her. She ground against his hand.

Her toes found a crack in the rock, giving her extra purchase against him. His mouth was hot against her lower back as his fingers worked in her. The water lapped against her like a tongue, and she could not tell if it was its natural movement or if he had ordered the water to please her so. She felt the pleasure building inside of her, hot, swirling, and she wanted to draw it all up inside of her, keep it forever, make it last her whole life long. She did not want to go over the edge, because then it would end. Alexandra turned her head, moaning and biting into her own arm, trying to hold on, to the feeling and to him.

Triton slipped a second finger into her, moving them like a pair of shears. Alexandra swore into her arm. His fingers were so big, so powerful. How could she bear it? She squeezed her muscles to draw him in deeper.

Triton snuck a hand to her breast, rolled her nipple between his fingers. "Bear down," he ordered.

The water lapped harder against her. Alexandra shook her head.

"Bear down," he repeated, sinking his teeth into her shoulder blade. "I order you to bear down."

Alexandra obeyed, closed her eyes, and bore down on his fingers. The water swirled against her, within her, around her. She could not tell if she was the water or if she was herself, all she knew was that she was like a giant wave—drawn up and up to a great height, and then she came crashing down. And all was still.

Alexandra's eyes fluttered open, a slight sting of salt water in her vision. She flexed her fingers against the rock. It was still there. She could count her breaths. She could feel the heat of Triton on her back, but she herself felt she was made of lightning, crackling from head to toe.

Triton kissed her cheek. "Good girl." He brushed a few

strands of hair out of her eyes. Alexandra nodded. *I am very good. I am very, very good.*

Triton wrapped his arms around her waist, caught her lips in his. His kiss was slow, steady, meant to keep a fire burning. He rocked against Alexandra, tilting her hips so she could feel the hard ridge of him, hidden beneath his tail, sliding against her.

"Do you want me?" he asked.

"Yes." She was still quivering from her orgasm but already aching to feel him again.

Triton nudged her legs open a little wider. Alexandra's nipples brushed against the rough rock, but she didn't care. His big hands clasped over hers, warm and soothing in their possessiveness. *A king doesn't grasp anything he doesn't want.* Triton moved against her, the tip of him sliding inside of her, as if he unfurled his length within her. She gave out a small moan.

Triton tilted her hips so her breasts were held apart from the rock while her hands remain firmly affixed. He moved within her, using his powerful tail to keep himself above the water while he drove himself in her. Alexandra felt the slickness of him against the backs of her thighs. She had imagined it would feel like touching a whale or a dolphin, not that she had ever been that close to either, so she was surprised that it felt so natural. It was like moving against a solid wave, a wave that had heft. A wave that was cool against her but hot within her.

A breeze played along the sides of her breasts, but the only sound was Triton's breath hot against her ear. Even the waves had gone quiet. All the sea was focused on the movement of his body along hers, on the single focus of him, thrusting in her, on the heat building within her. They were like the eye of a storm, calm, powerful, crackling with energy.

Triton shifted, increased his pace, and now the two of them moved like thunder, galloping together from a rumble to a crash. Their moans came faster, the need within them building. Although she knew the golden cuffs wouldn't let her go anywhere, Alexandra gripped onto the rock. The heat within her was building, too much, too fast.

I'm only human. What if I cannot take it?

Triton intertwined his fingers with hers, squeezing her hand, slamming into her, fierce and steady. It was this gesture, reassurance mixed with dominance, that sent her over the edge. Her orgasm rolled through her, coming like the surf, set after set. All she could do was hang onto Triton and ride it, gasping, sobbing, while the sea king thundered within her. She was tumbling through space and time, only vaguely aware of the rock beneath her, the wind in her hair, salt stinging her lips. There was a crack of lightning, a surge of heat, and a roar from Triton that showed he had tumbled over the edge too. She rode one final wave of pleasure as Triton throbbed within her. Everything in her quivered, and if not for the golden cuffs, she would have sunk into the sea. Through her haze, she felt the last delicious drag as he softened and tucked back into himself.

The next thing she felt was Triton's kisses on her cheek. He unlocked the golden cuffs, wrapped her in his arms. They were moving through the water, and then they were back on the beach. Triton curled her against his chest, winding his hands in her hair, murmuring sweet things to her. Alexandra wrapped one hand in his beard, drawing him to her lips.

"That was indeed very, very different," she gasped.

Triton's laugh was deep, and low. High above them, a shooting star fell through the sky.

A SHORT TIME LATER, Alexandra awoke on the beach, curled in the warm shelter of Triton's body.

He hasn't disappeared.

Far away, a clock struck ten. Out of habit, Alexandra thought sleepily, *Time for second intermission.*

She stretched and burrowed closer to Triton's chest. His hand lay across her hip, his thumb lightly caressing her. Alexandra opened her eyes to see him gazing tenderly at her. The soft glow in his eyes was so sweet, it made her think he could possibly be more human than deity. She had read that the gods, even the lesser deities, could be mercurial and cruel. Although she had fully experienced him in his mer-form, he had shown her more humanity, kindness, and care than any other being in Monte Carlo. Well, perhaps chaining her to the rock had been a bit possessive, but she had asked for it.

"You are beautiful when you sleep," said Triton.

Alexandra beamed. She felt like the most powerful person on earth. A king had risen out of the water, seen her dance, and chosen her for his lover. If she was good enough for a sea deity, then surely no one could refuse her.

Alexandra thought of Madame and her garish rouge, of the sinewy dance master whose face sagged like the molted shell of a crab. Who were they to deny her? Who were they to reject a dance that had pleased a sea king? Who were they to deny the people the pleasure of watching a dance loved by the gods?

It was only second intermission. Alexandra sat upright. She could still make the third act.

6

A GIFT FREELY GIVEN

*W*hen Alexandra abruptly sat upright, Triton looked about for a threat.

"What is it? What's wrong?" Triton was alarmed. He had not detected any danger, yet she looked startled. Her eyes searched the beach, the color high on her cheeks.

"Nothing's wrong. I must go. Have you seen my clothing?" She moved to rise. Triton held her by the wrists.

"Why must you go now? What's happened?"

Alexandra held his hands, her smile wide, her words tumbling over each other. "Nothing has happened. Or, rather, *you* happened. The bells—it's ten o'clock. I can still make the third act. I can still dance!"

"But you said you could not dance…" Triton held fast to her hands. He did not want to let her go.

"They wouldn't let me. But you said it yourself—they are fools. They wouldn't let me dance, but that is only because I was waiting for their permission. I can't wait any longer. I have to make them let me. If my dancing pleased you, the king of the sea, it will be good enough for crowds of Monte Carlo."

"And if they forbid you to perform?"

"Then I will find another way. I don't need them in order to be free." Alexandra's chin was high, her eyes bright. She glowed with confidence.

Her demeanor reminded Triton of his youngest daughter, burning to rush headlong into the future. His daughter was still asking his permission, his blessing, but soon she might find another way, a way would not include him. As afraid as he was of losing his daughter to a human, he was more afraid of losing her completely. He could either help her make a way or she would find a way around him. If anything, his daughter was as headstrong as he was. It was in everyone's best interests if he let both Alexandra and Amarine go.

Triton's arms fell to his sides. Alexandra turned from him, squinting to see her clothing. She would return to her life, and he to his. He did not want this to be the end of it, but he didn't know how to preserve their connection. He had always been the one to choose when and where his affairs happened; he was always the one to summon and arrange. The first to leave, never to return. His self-preservation came from his freedom to vanish. Once hunted by humans, he had learned never to be beckoned. And yet how could he find Alexandra again if she could not call?

"The stories are true," she said, holding up her discarded boots. "Once you meet a god, you'll be forever changed. Alas, I won't be able to tell anyone why I'm changed."

"You won't tell anyone?" Triton felt something silent within him begin to sputter to life.

"Of course not." She cocked her head, her sincerity disarming him. "You're a secret I want all to myself."

A secret. She didn't want him as a trophy, a prize fish for her wall. She wanted him for herself, because he was a myth come true. Something to believe in. Could he believe too?

"I want to give you a gift," said Triton. With a turn of his trident, a beautiful, long pearl necklace appeared in his hand, shining just like the moon, just like her eyes. "Take this necklace, and think of me. If you twist the strands together like so"—Triton twisted the necklace in a three-step spiral—"I will know that you are calling for me, and I will come."

Alexandra fingered the luminous orbs of the necklace, her brow creasing.

"You don't like it?" Triton drew the necklace back against him.

Alexandra's eyes glistened, and her voice caught with emotion. "No, I love it. I love it so much. It reminds me of something that was taken from me.

"This necklace can't be lost, or stolen. I will always know where it is," he said.

"You would give this to me? And I could call you? You won't…disappear?"

Triton's voice deepened, as if making a momentous proclamation. "If you are willing to meet me, I will come." Alexandra was biting her lip; what did that mean? Would she accept? Or would he be made a fool again?

She nodded slowly, her smile spreading over him like the sun. He could have fallen to his knees, he was so grateful.

Triton placed the necklace on her, fingering the pearls along her collarbone as they dipped into the valley between her breasts. He twisted her nipple between two pearls and was rewarded by her sharp intake of breath. He cupped her breast. "There are many ways I would like to see you," he murmured. "I cannot leave my kingdom for long, but I can certainly leave on a full moon night."

Alexandra placed her hand over his and drew his palm to her heart. "If you are willing to return, I am willing to call you. I will come to you every full moon, for as long as you want to see me." She tilted her head to kiss him, and he pulled her closer to him.

Triton took his time with their embrace, savoring the lushness of her body in his arms, the taste of her on his lips. This wonderful, beautiful human, who had been such a surprise to him. He had come to the shore looking for revenge, but he had found something more powerful. Redemption. A safe heaven for his heart and his body. An opportunity to salvage his relationship with his daughter. He had found something that belonged completely to him, that had nothing to do with the responsibilities he bore in the world below, that he did not have to share or involve in his calculations for the wellbeing of his people. Something he could have, simply because he wanted it. *Her.*

Triton released Alexandra. She rose, gathered the remnants of her garments. She held up the wrecked corset and quirked an eyebrow at him. "You are nothing if not thorough," she said.

Being a king, Triton did not shrug, but he delivered his joke with the aplomb of the most experienced stage bawd. "I come by my aversion to hooks honestly."

Alexandra laughed as she wrapped her shawl around her body. She hugged the half-empty wine bottle to her chest.

"Good luck," said Triton.

Alexandra gave him a mischievous smile. "If they try to stop me, I will tell them I know someone who can make a tidal wave."

Triton threw his head back and laughed, and that was how she left him, chuckling on the beach, watching her make her way toward the glittering lights of the opera house. Triton retreated to the warmth of the water, not wanting to leave until she was out of sight. At the edge of the sand, Alexandra turned around. She gave a twist of the necklace, and Triton felt it tug at his heart. In answer, he twirled his trident, sending a glowing path of iridescence from the water, straight to her feet. Alexandra blew him a kiss and walked away.

Triton dove beneath the waves and surged toward home. He would be back on the next full moon, if not sooner. But right now, he had to have an urgent discussion with his daughter. He also had a few new decrees to make, judicious decrees, regarding interactions between the mer-world and the human world. It would take some thought, and some planning, but there must be a safer way, for them all. Before tonight, he had thought the most treacherous thing was a human heart. Now he knew that a heart that lacked compassion was far more treacherous. Triton swam with vigor, and for the first time since he had become a single parent, he felt a little bit of hope for his daughters. The shores of love were most treacherous when they were forbidden. He would help them navigate those waters, turn a tempest into a refuge.

I know what will be the perfect wedding gift for my girl, thought Triton. *Her very own pair of legs.*

EPILOGUE

*A*nd that, my darlings, was how Alexandra arrived onstage, damp from the water and still warm from the sea king's embrace, draped in a shawl and a pearl necklace.

That was also how Alexandra, La Sirène de Monte Carlo, the most celebrated act in the early days of the Opéra de Monte Carlo, was born. When Sandra Bernhardt danced as a water nymph, it was as homage to what she had seen on that stage. Alexandra La Sirène was an international sensation, revered by the crowned heads of Europe. No one could say where she had learned her craft, but there were many who tried to tell the tale.

There were also stories of a nearby kingdom that had gained a mysterious new princess who had appeared on the beach one day "as if risen from the sea." It was rumored she had once been a mermaid, for ever since she had arrived, the kingdom's fishing nets were perpetually full and their waters calm. At sunset, there could be seen a tail splashing on the horizon, and they called it "Triton's salute."

Speaking of Triton's salute, the royal box in the Opéra de Monte Carlo was said to often host a mysterious, silver-haired figure. During the performances of La Sirène, the bracing air of the sea would waft throughout the opera house. La Sirène was so celebrated that when she refused to perform on the night of the full moon, no one questioned her. Not a creature in the world could deny her or her glinting pearl necklace.

And that is how, on many a moonlit night, tucked into a Mediterranean cove, Triton and Alexandra could find each other, again, and again, and again.

That is the end of this tale, mes chers, but there are more to come. On a remote tropical island, an exiled mermaid and a castaway cowboy wait for their chance at love...but I shall save that for another time.

Raise your glass, toast your lovers, and remember: we are all worthy of love, even when we are half-fish.

AMOUR, amour, always amour....

MADAME DE BOUDOIR

❀

BONUS CHAPTER FROM KING OF THE SEA

One month after their first encounter, Alexandra waits for Triton by the shore. Will Triton heed her call?

Get the bonus chapter at http://bit.ly/lovelyreaderbonus!

SNEAK PEEK: PRINCESS OF THE SEA

A LITTLE MERMAID'S ROYAL WEDDING

The Sea of Love Series continues with Book 2!

IT'S A RECURRING DREAM I'VE HAD, ever since I left the sea to be with my prince. Only this time, it ends differently.

My wedding is to be the largest this kingdom has seen in generations. People line the streets, cheering and celebrating. Every public house is overrun with patrons. Merchants hawk sweets and ribbons tied to sticks, which children beg their parents to purchase for them. Even from within the Great Hall, where my prince and I entertain our guests, we can hear the cheers waft through the palace's walls. They have needed a reason to celebrate. It has been gloomy since the death of their queen, some years prior. That is one thing my prince and I have in common. We have our love, of course, but also the loss of our mothers. I kiss my prince and feel that I have everything I wanted. It has been worth it, to leave the sea and make my home here. Nothing can go wrong.

Then the dream shifts.

My father arrives in the Great Hall with all five of my mer-sisters, half the sea king's royal court, and a myriad of our relatives, some of them ancient and half-immortal, all of them very magical. They are all also dripping wet and nude.

I am horrified.

Suddenly, it is quite clear that I have made a horrible mistake. How could I have ever thought the prince and I could make a life together?

All my grand visions for myself crumble. There will be no swimming back and forth to Triton's golden palace whenever I please, or bringing my sisters to the castle, showing them the gardens and the surrounding villages. I had hoped we would even ride horses! Mermaids on horses! My sisters would have found it hilarious and wonderful.

But here is the stark reality, right before my face, in the form of a soggy sea court splashing through the Great Hall, eager to meet my husband's family, while the humans recoil in horror. Against the dank stone of this seaside castle, my usually glorious family appears like salt-stained beasts sent to ruin the furniture.

And it's my fault. I hadn't told them about the secret chest of garments I kept in the cove, so I could be dressed when I reappeared in the castle. I hadn't shown them of the back entrances I used, so no one would know I had gone for a swim, so no one would witness my tail give way to legs upon my return, so no one would see how I lingered at water's edge and swallowed my tears when I left the sea. I hadn't taught them the customs of my fiancé and his family. "Arrive before sunset on the first day of the full moon! It will be a grand party!" I'd said. Like an idiot. An unfeeling, thought-less, reckless, inconsiderate *idiot*.

Ignominious droplets fall from my father's powerful

trident to the floor. My sisters' usually shimmering hair sags on their shoulders. They are soggy, limp, and bewildered. They look amongst their surroundings with blurry eyes and teeter on wobbly legs, these creatures who can swim leagues and fight monsters with ease now fumble through a foreign element that I had neglected to prepare them for—just as I'd failed to prepare *it* for *them*.

I had done this to them, to those who had traveled so far for me. As if I had not a care for those who cared so much for me.

I look to my prince, desperate for help. He turns away from me, his shoulders hunched in shame.

"Please," I say. "Help them. They're wet."

My sisters stumble toward me. Their legs begin to crumble, their dried flesh rips away as they fall to the ground. They crawl toward me, dragging a pile of brittle fish bones behind them. "Amarine! Why have you left us? Help us!" they beg.

Someone in the crowd begins to scream. Shrieks of horror quickly turn to rage. "Monsters!" they yell. "Princess of Death!" shouts another. A thrown object sails through the air and bounces off my father's shoulder. Triton's eyes glow like fire, his power growing. He grows taller and taller, the fire pours from his eyes, burning the people closest to him. The fire sweeps the room, consuming everything, beginning with my prince. My father's rage knows no bounds. Everyone will be consumed. Now there will be war. Nothing good can survive this.

My beautiful wedding gown goes up in smoke, and soon I too am consumed.

I wake with a start, silken sheets tumbling to the floor. The early morning breeze flutters the gauzy curtains along my arched balcony door. I can see dawn's first light creeping over the horizon. I look beside me, where my prince still sleeps, his hand resting on my hip. Even in sleep, Caspian can't bear to be separated from me. He has his own chambers but sneaks into mine each night, despite the way Sir Maurice, the head courtier, sniffs about "propriety" and "appearances."

I slip from the bed, tiptoe past the dog—sweet, slobbery Samson—who snores from his cushion on the floor. I push the curtains aside to step onto my balcony. Below me, gentle waves lap the stone foundations of the castle. A fresh morning breeze dances over my flesh. I long to feel the water on my skin instead.

I look upon the wide expanse of the sea, searching for something familiar, a telltale break in the surface, a darting bit of shimmer, anything that would signify that one of my own kind is nearby. But there is no one to comfort me. There is only the ocean, my first home.

I close my eyes and send my thoughts into the water. If only one of my sisters were nearby enough to feel me. I make inaudible clicks with my tongue. I know those sound waves won't reach far enough, but I try anyway. At this moment, I feel nothing but despair.

I'm sorry. Forgive me. Please don't hate me. Please let it all be well.

I open my eyes and immediately feel ashamed. I shouldn't feel despair. After all, it is the day before my wedding. Early sunlight glints on the water's surface, as if to reassure me that everything is, indeed, all sunshine.

It's very bizarre to be marrying a human.

I didn't mean to fall in love, I swear. With a human, especially one who was a prince. It would have been easier to fall in love with a fisherman if I was going to break all the rules for a land spouse. An easier life, an easier time keeping my secrets.

I've been keeping so many secrets, mostly from the humans. Unwise as it may be, Caspian and I had entrusted a few intimates with the truth of my origin. Yet even with that knowledge, no one truly comprehends how bewildering this life is to me. I sit through their lengthy meals, gaze at their many paintings, and jostle in carriages through their lands. I smile as if I understand everything. Truly, I understand nothing. It is all foreign to me. My sweet prince tries to explain, to draw me in, to make every adjustment easier on me. I want to please him, so I pretend that the transition is seamless, that adaptation is painless. But it is only when I swim that I can fully be myself.

When I swim, my worries fall away. I don't think of the massive amounts of upheaval I have brought to my life—and to this kingdom and mine. I don't think about my anger with my father's attempts to control me. I don't think about my encounter with the sea witch Sidra. I certainly don't think about how foolish I was to ask a sea witch for a spell that would cloak my whereabouts—so my father wouldn't know I'd run off to be with my prince. I wince, forcing myself not to think of how I had almost bartered away my voice. For no one wins when you bargain with a sea witch.

When I swim, I don't think about the moment my father burst into the sea witch's lair, foiled her spell, reconciled with me, then gave me his blessing and accompanied me to the shore to meet the man I love. When I swim, I don't think about how I miss my family. I don't think about the pinch of jealousy I had when I met my father's human love, Alexandra. I don't think of the ache that accompanies my happiness for him, because while I want him to be happy, I will always miss my mother. When I swim, all of these jumbled feelings are merely a part of the adventure of falling love.

When I'm not swimming, I'm worried there are fish bones under my nails or a scale flake on my face. I'm worried a fisherman might see me at a vulnerable moment, caught between sea and land. I'm worried I will misinterpret the use of various human objects and betray my origins to the wrong person at the wrong time. I'm worried my true nature will overtake me, that I'll encounter water at an inopportune time or, worse, my temper will betray me. The wife my prince is expected to have, from what I understand, is a docile, supportive creature. I am not. According to human lore, a mermaid is a hybrid—part-fish and all monster. According to their stories, monsters ruin everything.

I try not to think of it. I try to focus on the extreme bliss of being in love.

My strategy, so far, has been to keep my worlds separate. I slip away from my prince when I feel my mer-form about to burst through the surface. I share with him only the most whimsical and magical parts of my mermaid life: stories of racing dolphin pods, of leaping over waves in the moonlight, of singing with my sisters, of sneaking to the surface to feel the sun on my face. I don't tell him that yesterday I punched an impudent shark in the face. I don't tell him how my father can send lightning through the water. I don't tell him how, with a lilt in my song, I've enchanted many a creature into doing exactly what I want. He knows nothing of my real power.

I only slip into the sea once a day, to clear my head, to swim fast, to move with the rhythms that feel the most natural to me. In the world above, they move like the ticks on a clock, the day pushing forward like a crab inching up a rock. I need to feel the rush and swell of the ocean to feel like myself. I need its expanse, its oblivion, to be able to find myself, to know that I am still Amarine, daughter of Triton, maid of the sea.

I had thought I could slip in and out of the ocean at will. But what will happen when my sea life comes to me?

I've never even showed him my tail. It's as if I think I'm a sea witch, and all I have to do is enchant him until the wedding, until it's too late for him to reject me.

As the day grows brighter, it becomes clearer to me that there will be no hiding my world from him. How long could I keep a secret anyway, before it pushed itself between us? How long can I keep a secret about myself, when I have invited the very secret to our wedding?

When my family arrives, he'll know. My world could drown him. My family could kill him. To me, we are strong, fierce, and magnificent. But what looks like magic to me could look like duplicity to him. I may hope he'd see us as divine, but he may also see us as monstrous. And monsters ruin everything.

Would it be better if I left now? Would Caspian be safer if he never married me? If I jumped into the sea now, I could meet up with my family, head them off before they arrived. I could be a minor interference in my prince's life's story. If I went home now, he would have a chance to marry someone who wouldn't destroy him.

The sea begins to turn from silver to blue as the sun rises, reminding me of the flash in Sidra's eyes as we escaped her lair. The last thing she'd shouted lingers still in my mind, as much as I fight to forget it.

He cannot love what he cannot understand.

Was it a curse, or a prophecy? Was there time to save my family, myself, my love?

The salt sprays against the castle walls. I wanted so badly to know the world above. I gave up my life within the sea to come here. Am I trapped now? Are we all doomed?

Find out what happens next for Princess Amarine and her royal wedding to Prince Caspian in Princess of the Sea, *now available at your favorite retailer or at lauralovelybooks.com!*

SNEAK PEEK: SPLASH ME

A SPLASH-INSPIRED ROMANCE

"What's your fantasy? One that you never told anyone?" he asks.

Kevin and I have had five dates—and sex twice. He is big-hearted and big-boned, with a slightly ragged haircut and a laugh that reminds me of the luckdragon in *The Neverending Story*. I like him so much, even though he's a total dweeb.

I stare at the dirty text for one minute. Then two.

My fantasy? I take a swig of wine. Should I cop out? Make a joke about a naughty nurse? Or do I risk being completely honest...

If I tell him the truth, I think he would make it good.

I know he'll make it good. I take a deep breath—I'm all in.

I text back, "Have you seen the movie *Splash*?"

SPLASH ME is available now!

Laura Lovely's Fairytale Remixes are short hot-n-humorous standalones, inspired by fairytales, mythology and pop culture.

AUTHOR'S NOTE

Merci, merci. Grazie. Danke. Mahalo. You are too kind. Thank you for reading. What clever beauties you are.

I have long loved Hans Christian Andersen's *The Little Mermaid*, and adore Disney's film of the same name. But often I have found myself wondering what happened to the family and the world the little mermaid was so eager to leave behind? Thank you for the opportunity to explore what lies beyond the stories we already know.

This is a work of historical fantasy. Although I was inspired by the history of the Opéra de Monte Carlo, I used it more as a jumping off point than a structuring event. Nothing about this story is false, but not all of it may be true. *C'est la vie.* Don't worry about it too much. Worry is the enemy of love, and all I want for you is love.

ACKNOWLEDGMENTS

This publication would not have been possible without the encouragement and guidance of the magical boss unicorns known as HBIC Nation. My everlasting gratitude and devotion goes to Alexis Anne, Lindsay Emory, Mary-Chris Escobar, Julia Kelly, and the glitterrific land-mermaid, Alexandra Haughton. All my love goes to my beautiful editor, Mayumi Shimose Poe. We've come a long way since reading Nora Roberts aloud to each other in our lingerie. Additionally, the face of this book would be a far lesser masterpiece without the efforts of my brain-twin, Romanced by the Cover.

Others who have supported this work include: Erin Clark, Elizabeth Barrett Groth, Michael Levinton, Kat Reaney, Kate Scelsa, Luke Stoffel, Nani Sugar, Nate Sykes, Khaliah Williams, Eve Wolff, Sweet Baby Frannie, and the Romance Writers of America.

I am also extremely grateful for my fans and readers, who possess unparalleled amounts of brain and beauty. I know of no greater companions to join me in these many adventures. Keep sending me all the mermaid paraphernalia you see. I think of you often, as well.

ABOUT THE AUTHOR

She's got style, she's got grace, she's probably got glitter on her face. A mermaid expert and folklore enthusiast, Laura Lovely is the author of award-winning steamy paranormal romances, usually featuring mermaids and mermen. She also writes short contemporary romances inspired by fairytales, mythology and pop culture.

An avid traveler, Laura Lovely is permanently jet-lagged and always looking forward to her next escape. Laura Lovely is at her best when listening to power ballads, watching romantic comedies and sipping champagne.

For updates, giveaways and behind the scenes exclusives, please join my email list at lauralovelybooks.com/newsletter.

lauralovelybooks.com

ABOUT THE NARRATOR

Madame de Boudoir is the narrator, chanteuse and hostess of the Sea of Love series. A daughter of Aphrodite, she was discovered as an infant in a trunk of pearls and raised among the ball gowns in the wardrobe departments of the greatest opera houses of Europe. On many a moonlit night, she can be found at the shore, listening to the tales of her merfolk relatives, which she is glad to share with you. As a mistress of ceremonies, she is known for her opulent costumes, revealing stories, and flights of fancy. Bridging the Gilded and the Digital Ages, Madame de Boudoir's stories are rich with extravagant feelings and historical fantasies. Madame wishes to remind you that: "We are all worthy of love, even when we are half fish."

facebook.com/lauralovelybooks

instagram.com/lauravonholt

bookbub.com/authors/laura-lovely

goodreads.com/lauralovelybooks

Made in the USA
Middletown, DE
15 September 2022